Railway Children

Written by E Nesbit

Retold by Harriet Castor

Illustrated by Rosalind Lyons

Collins

Chapter 1

They weren't railway children to begin with. They were just ordinary children, and they lived with their father and mother in a large redbrick house in the suburbs of London. There were three of them. The eldest was Roberta – Bobbie for short. Next came Peter, and the youngest was Phyllis.

These three lucky children had everything they needed: good clothes, warm fires and plenty of toys, a mother who made up funny pieces of poetry for their birthdays, and a father who was never cross, never unjust and always ready for a game.

They ought to have been very happy. And so they were, but they didn't know *how* happy until their life in the redbrick house was over and done with, and they had to live a very different life indeed.

The dreadful change came quite suddenly. Peter was celebrating his tenth birthday. They had games, a cake, and Peter was given a toy steam engine. The engine quickly got broken, but even that wasn't so bad, since Father was very clever at mending things and Peter knew he only needed to wait until after dinner and then everything would be put right.

But after dinner, just as Peter began to explain about his engine, there was a knock at the front door. A moment later the maid came in and said that two gentlemen wanted to see Father.

"Get rid of them quickly, dear, whoever they are," said Mother, as Father got out of his chair. "It's nearly the children's bedtime."

But Father couldn't get rid of them quickly. Peter, Bobbie and Phyllis waited a long time. They could hear Father talking to the gentlemen in another room, and his voice sounded louder than usual and different, somehow. After a while Mother went to join them, and there was more talking.

At last the children heard boots go out and down the front steps. "They're leaving!" said Phyllis with relief. The *clip-clop* of hooves echoed in the street outside as a horse-drawn cab drove away.

Then Mother came back into the room. Her face was as white as her lace collar, and her eyes looked very big and shining.

"Father's been called away – on business," she said. "Come, darlings, it's your bedtime."

"It wasn't bad news, Mummy, was it?" asked Bobbie a little later, when Mother came to give her a goodnight kiss. "Is anyone dead – or – "

"Nobody's dead – no," said Mother. "I can't tell you anything tonight, my pet. Go to sleep."

But Bobbie heard the catch in her mother's voice, and knew that she'd been crying. When Mother looked in much later that night, on her way to bed, Bobbie was still awake. She didn't want to add to her mother's worries, though, so she lay very still and said nothing.

Chapter 2

The next morning, when the children came down to breakfast, Mother had already gone out. It was seven in the evening before she got back, looking so ill and tired that the children felt they couldn't ask her any questions. She sank into an armchair and Peter fetched her soft velvety slippers.

When she'd had a cup of tea, Mother said, "Now, my darlings, I want to tell you something. Those men last night did bring very bad news, and Father will be away for some time. I'm very worried about it, and I want you all to help me by being good and happy and not arguing."

Bobbie and Peter exchanged guilty glances – they'd been having a row just before Mother arrived.

"We won't argue – we promise," they said.

"Then," Mother went on, "I don't want you to ask me questions about this trouble. Don't ask anybody else questions, either."

"Why not?" said Phyllis.

"Because you don't need to know anything about it," Mother replied. "It's business trouble. But don't *you* worry, my darlings. It'll all come right in the end."

For the next few weeks, life carried on almost as usual. The children went to school and came home, ate their meals, played with toys and went to bed at the usual times. But everything felt different now, because Mother was nearly always out, and Father wasn't there at all.

Then one morning, at breakfast, Mother said, "Everything's settled, my pets. We're going to leave this house, and go and live in the country."

A whirling week of packing followed – not just packing clothes, like when they went to the seaside, but packing chairs and tables, saucepans and blankets, crockery, carpets and candlesticks. The house was like a furniture warehouse, and the children enjoyed it very much, although it seemed to Bobbie that Mother chose all the plainest, ugliest furniture to take with them, and all the most beautiful furniture to leave behind.

"We must take what is useful," said Mother. "We've got to play at being poor for a bit."

The next day a horse-drawn cab came to take them all to the station. There, they boarded a steam train and set off on what turned out to be a long journey. By the time they reached their destination it was dark, and all three children had been asleep.

Standing on the draughty platform, they shivered and sneezed and hoped the walk to the new house wouldn't be long. Peter's nose was colder than it had ever been. Bobbie's hat was crooked, and the elastic seemed tighter than usual. Phyllis's shoelaces had come undone.

The walk turned out to be dark, muddy and almost all uphill. At last, when they'd left the road and crossed some fields, Mother pointed to a dark, lumpish thing up ahead. "That's the house," she said. "It's called Three Chimneys."

It didn't look welcoming – there were no lights in the windows. Mother unlocked the door and lit a match. By its thin little glimmer the children saw a bare kitchen with a stone floor. There were no curtains, no hearthrug and the fireplace showed only cold, dead ashes.

Mother touched the match to a candle on the kitchen table. The children looked at one another by its flickering light.

"What fun!" said Mother, smiling bravely and putting her arms around them all. "Haven't you often told me, darlings, that you'd like something to happen, like it does in stories? Well, now it has. This is quite an adventure, isn't it?"

Chapter 3

The house looked much better by daylight. When Bobbie and Phyllis went down to the yard next morning to wash at the pump – since Three Chimneys had no bathroom – they saw that the house was whitewashed and pretty, with a roof of mossy thatch. Beyond the yard they stood in, open fields stretched in every direction.

"This is *far* prettier than our old house," said Phyllis, pumping the water for Bobbie.

"And this is much more fun than washing indoors!" laughed Bobbie. "See how sparkly the wet stones look in the sunshine!"

When Peter was up and dressed, the three of them began to explore. The house stood on a hill. Down below they could see the line of the railway, and the black yawning mouth of a tunnel. The station was out of sight.

"Let's go down and look at the railway," said Peter. "There might be trains passing."

They ran downhill over smooth, short grass. The way ended in a steep slope and a wooden fence – and there was the railway with its shining rails and posts and signals.

Bobbie, Peter and Phyllis climbed on to the top of the fence. Suddenly a rumbling sound made them look along the line to the right, where the dark mouth of the tunnel opened in the face of a rocky cliff. The next moment a train rushed out of the tunnel with a shriek and a snort.

"Perhaps it's going where Father is!" cried Phyllis. "Let's wave and it'll take our love to him!"

They all pulled out their handkerchiefs and waved and waved.

And from a first-class carriage window, a hand waved back.

"Did you see that?" cried Peter, when the rush of the train's passing was over, and the pebbles on the line had stopped jumping and rattling.

"Yes, an old gentleman waved!" said Bobbie. "He had white hair and a top hat. He looked very nice."

"Do you think that train really *could* be going to where Father is?" asked Phyllis.

"I think Father must be in London," said Peter. "Let's go and ask at the station if that was the London train."

So they set off, following the direction of the railway line at a safe distance. It was a long walk but it was worth it. Never before had any of them arrived at a station in such an adventurous way – not through the front entrance, but by the sloping end of the platform. It was exciting, too, to pass close enough to a signal box to notice the wires, and to peep into the station porter's room, where the lamps were, and where the railway timetable hung on the wall.

Further along the platform they met the porter himself, who was very friendly. They learned several interesting things from him, including that his name was Mr Perks, and that the lamps at the front of engines are called headlights and the ones at the back tail-lights. They learned for the first time, too, that steam engines are not all alike.

"Alike?" said Perks. "No indeed! No more alike than you and me. The little one that went by just now – that was a tank. She's off to do some shunting. Then there are goods engines – great, strong things with three wheels each side. And then there are mainline engines – built for speed as well as power. The 9:15 – that train you saw a while ago – she's one of those."

"Was she going to London, Mr Perks?" asked Bobbie.

Perks said she was. The children agreed, on the long walk home, that they would wave to the 9:15 every morning.

And so they did. And every morning, the old gentleman in the first-class carriage waved back. The children liked to think that perhaps he knew Father, and would meet him "in business" – wherever that might be – and tell him how his three children stood by a railway line far away in the countryside and waved their love to him every morning, wet or fine.

Chapter 4

Spring turned into summer, and Bobbie, Peter and Phyllis kept up their habit of going each day to the railway. Perks the porter became a dear friend, and sometimes the children got a chance to speak to the stationmaster, too. He would come out from his important office behind the window where tickets were sold, and he would always be kind. One day he gave them each an orange, and promised to take them up into the signal box some time, when he wasn't so busy.

Meanwhile Mother worked hard every day, writing stories that she sold to magazines. She came downstairs at teatime and read aloud what she had written. They were lovely stories. But Bobbie, Peter and Phyllis thought it was a shame that she spent all day shut up in her room, and that she couldn't enjoy the rocks and hills and trees – and, above all, the railway – as they did.

Of course, they knew Mother had to work – to pay for the house, and the food and firewood they needed. The children often brought her little bunches of flowers they had picked, to say thank you. But they longed to be able to surprise her with something a bit different.

One day, Phyllis had the idea of picking wild cherries. They had seen the blossom on the trees in the spring, so they knew where to look for the fruit. The trees grew along the rocky face of the cliff where the tunnel-mouth was.

The tunnel was some way from Three Chimneys, so they told Mother they were going for a picnic and would be out all day. Mother lent them her watch so that they wouldn't be late for tea.

When the children got to the top of the cutting, where a channel had been cut into the hill to make way for the railway line, they leaned over the fence and looked down. The sides of the cutting were made of grey rock, and in cracks here and there, bushes and trees had taken root. Near the tunnel was a flight of steep wooden steps leading down to the line.

"Let's climb down," said Peter. "I'm sure the cherries will be quite easy to reach from the steps."

So they made their way towards the steps.

Suddenly Bobbie said, "Hush. Stop! What's that?"

"That" was a very odd noise indeed – a sort of rustling, whispering sound. As they listened, it grew louder and more rumbling.

"Look!" cried Peter. "The tree over there!"

The tree he pointed at was moving – all in one piece, as though it were a live creature and were walking down the side of the cutting.

"It's magic," said Phyllis breathlessly.

Now several trees on the opposite bank seemed to be slowly walking towards the railway line. Stones and loose earth fell and rattled on the rails far below.

"It's *all* coming down," Peter tried to say, but he found there was hardly any voice to say it with. And just as he spoke the rocks and trees and bushes, with a rushing sound, slipped right away from the face of the cutting and fell on the line with a blundering crash. A cloud of dust rose up.

"Look what a great mound it's made!" said Bobbie.

"Yes, it's fallen right across the line," said Phyllis.

"The 11:29 train hasn't gone by yet," said Peter. "We must let them know at the station, or there'll be a dreadful accident."

"Let's run!" said Bobbie, and began.

But Peter cried, "Come back!" and looked at Mother's watch. His face was whiter than they'd ever seen it.

"We won't get there in time," he said. "It's two miles away, and it's already past eleven."

"Then we must wave at the train when it comes, to stop it," said Bobbie, beginning to climb down the steep stairs.

"They'll just think it's *us*, as usual," said Phyllis, following. "We've waved so often before."

"If we only had something red to wave, like a flag," said Peter. "Everyone knows red means 'stop'."

Bobbie turned at the bottom of the stairs.

"But we do!" she cried. "Phyllis – our petticoats are red! Let's take them off."

They ran along the railway to the corner that would give them the best view of an oncoming train. There, they ripped the petticoats into six flag-sized pieces, and poked sharp sticks through the fabric to make flagpoles.

Two of the flags were set up in heaps of loose stones near the line. Then Phyllis and Peter each took a flag, and Bobbie took the remaining two, and they stood ready to wave them as soon as the train came in sight.

The children waited. The minutes ticked by so slowly that it seemed to Bobbie they had been standing there for hours and hours. And then came the distant rumble and hum of the metal, and a puff of white steam showed far away along the stretch of line.

"Stand firm," said Peter, "and wave like mad! When it gets to that big gorse bush, step back, but go on waving! Don't stand near the line, Bobbie!"

The steam train came rattling along very fast.

"They won't see us! It's all no good!" cried Bobbie.

The two little flags on the line swayed as the nearing train shook and loosed the heaps of stones that held them up. It seemed that the train came on as fast as ever. It was very near now.

"It's no good," Bobbie said again.

"Stand back!" shouted Peter suddenly, and he dragged Phyllis back by the arm.

The front of the engine looked black and enormous.

"Stop, stop, stop!" cried Bobbie. No one heard her. The oncoming rush of the train covered the sound of her voice. But afterwards she wondered whether the great engine itself had heard – for it slowed suddenly, slowed and stopped.

A moment later Bobbie was lying on the ground with her hands still gripping the sticks of the little red flags. She had fainted clean away.

Chapter 5

Bobbie, Peter and Phyllis had saved many lives that day. To thank them, the railway company organised a celebration at the station. There were lots of flowers, and a carpet had been put down, as if they were royalty.

Then one of the directors of the railway company made a speech – and it was their very own old gentleman, who always waved from his carriage! He said how brave the children had been, and gave them each a beautiful gold watch, with their names engraved inside.

The crowd – which included many of the passengers whose lives they had saved – clapped and cheered. It was a wonderful day – "The proudest day of our lives!" said Peter.

That night, as she settled to sleep, Bobbie thought about something she would have liked to tell the old gentleman. But it had been too public an occasion – she hadn't dared.

The truth was that Bobbie was thinking a great deal about Father. She'd tried not to wonder what the great trouble was, but she couldn't always help it. Father wasn't dead – Mother had said so. And he wasn't ill, or Mother would have been with him. So what was wrong?

It wasn't long afterwards that Bobbie found out a terrible secret.

Peter was recovering from an illness, and he was finding it very boring being stuck in bed. "Perks has a whole heap of magazines that people have left behind on trains," said Bobbie. "I'll go and ask him for some."

At the station, she found Perks busy cleaning lamps, but he was happy to help her. He fetched a big pile of magazines for Peter, and wrapped them up in newspaper and string.

"There!" he said. "That'll make them easier to carry."

"Thank you!" said Bobbie. She took the parcel, and started for home.

The magazines were heavy, and when she had to wait at a level crossing for a train to go by, she rested the parcel on top of the gate. She began to read the newspaper that the parcel was wrapped in.

Suddenly she clutched the parcel tighter and bent her head over it. It seemed like some horrible dream. She never remembered how she got home. But she tiptoed to her room and undid the parcel and read that printed column again, sitting on the edge of her bed, her hands and feet icy cold and her face burning.

What she read was headed, "End of the Spy Trial. Verdict. Sentence."

The name of the man who had been tried was the name of her father. The verdict was "Guilty". And the sentence was "Five years in jail".

"Oh, Daddy," she whispered, crushing the paper hard. "It's not true – I don't believe it. You never did! Never, never, never!"

Chapter 6

Now Bobbie knew the secret. A sheet of old newspaper wrapped round a parcel – just a little chance like that – had given the secret to her. Peter and Phyllis could see that Bobbie was upset about something, but she wouldn't say what. *Mother doesn't want us to know,* Bobbie thought. *I can't possibly tell them.*

There was only one person she felt she could tell – in fact, she *must* tell. So Bobbie wrote a letter to the old gentleman.

My Dear Friend -
You see what this paper says. It isn't true. Father isn't a spy and he never sold state secrets – he couldn't do such a thing. You are so good and clever – can you find out who really did it? Then they will let Father out of prison. Oh, please help me. Think if it was your daddy, how you would feel.
From Bobbie, with best love.

She cut the report out of the newspaper, and put it in the envelope with her letter. Then she took it down to the station. She asked Perks to give the letter to the old gentleman the next morning when the 9:15 train made its stop.

The weeks passed, and Bobbie heard no news. Her hopes sank lower and lower each day. It seemed there was nothing even the kind old gentleman could do to help Father, now that he was in jail.

When September came, Mother started teaching the children school lessons. They became so busy, they stopped going to the railway each day.

"I wonder if it misses us," said Phyllis at breakfast one morning. "We never go to see it now."

"The thing I don't like," said Bobbie, "is that we've stopped sending our love to Father by the 9:15 train."

"Then let's begin again – today!" said Peter.

The harebells and wild roses looked beautiful in the autumn sunshine as they walked down the slope to the railway. Bobbie stopped and gathered a handful of flowers.

"Hurry up, both of you," said Peter, "or we'll miss it!"

"Oh, bother!" said Phyllis. "My shoelace has come undone *again*!"

"Look!" cried Peter. "The signal's down. We must run!"

They ran. And once more they waved their handkerchiefs to the 9:15.

"Take our love to Father!" cried Bobbie. And the others, too, shouted – "Take our love to Father!"

The old gentleman waved from his first-class carriage window. There was nothing odd in that – he always waved. But what *was* strange was that from every window handkerchiefs fluttered, newspapers signalled, hands waved wildly. The train swept by with a roar, and the children were left looking at each other.

"What on earth does *that* mean?" asked Peter.

"I don't know," said Bobbie. "Perhaps the old gentleman told the people at his station to look out for us and wave. He knew we'd like it!"

The children walked home to begin their lessons. But that morning, Bobbie found she couldn't concentrate.

"Don't you feel well?" Mother asked, seeing her struggle with a very simple sum.

"I don't know," said Bobbie. "It isn't that I'm lazy ... Mother, will you let me off lessons today? I'd like to be by myself."

Mother said yes, and let Bobbie go outside, to see if the fresh air would clear her head.

I'll go down to the station, Bobbie said to herself, *and talk to Perks.*

She walked to the station, as if she were in a dream. There was no one on the platform at first – but then, when a train was signalled, Perks appeared. He hurried up to her and said, "Here you are! I've seen it in the paper and I don't think I was ever so glad of anything!"

"Seen *what* in the paper?" asked Bobbie, but already the train was steaming into the station and her words were drowned out by its noise.

Only three people got out of the train. The first was a farmer with two heavy baskets; the second was the grocer's wife, with a tin box and three brown paper parcels; and the third –

"Oh! My Daddy, my Daddy!" That scream went like a knife into the heart of everyone on the train, and people put their heads out of the windows. They saw a tall man and a young girl clinging to him, while his arms went tightly round her.

"Didn't Mother get my letter?" Father asked, as they went up the road.

"There weren't any letters this morning. Oh, Daddy! It *is* really you, isn't it?"

The clasp of his hand told her that it was.

"Everything's all right now, Bobbie. They've caught the man who really was the spy. Everyone knows now that it wasn't me."

"*I* always knew it wasn't," said Bobbie. "That's what I said to our old gentleman."

"Yes," said Father, "it's all his doing. And yours – my own little girl!" He stopped to give her another hug. Then he explained how the dear old gentleman had suspected all along that he was innocent, and had begun to investigate the case even before Bobbie had written her letter. At last the old gentleman had found the evidence that was needed to set Father free.

Feeling fit to burst with happiness, Bobbie took Father's hand again, and together they walked across the field. When they came close to the house, she ran ahead and flung open the door, calling back over her shoulder, "Come in, Daddy, come in!"

Father went in eagerly. Outside, the sun shone warmly on the green-gold spikes of grass and the harebells and wild roses. But it shone most warmly of all on the white house called Three Chimneys, where everyone was happy now.

All change!

RICH   POOR

TOWN   COUNTRY

DANGER   SAFETY

GUILTY   NOT GUILTY

SAD   HAPPY

Ideas for reading

Written by Clare Dowdall, PhD
Lecturer and Primary Literacy Consultant

Reading objectives:
- draw inferences such as inferring characters' feelings, thoughts and motives from their actions, and justify inferences with evidence
- predict what might happen from details stated and implied
- identify how language, structure and presentation contribute to meaning
- explain and discuss their understanding of what they have read
- provide reasoned justifications for their views

Spoken language objectives:
- participate in discussions, presentations, performances, role play, improvisations and debates

Curriculum links: History – local study; Geography – human geography

Resources: local maps; ICT; pens and paper

Build a context for reading
- Look at the front cover and ask children to describe what they can see happening. Focus on what's being waved and why.
- Ask children to approximate when the story is set and to justify their answers with evidence.
- Read the blurb. Ask children to suggest where Father has gone, and why the family has to move to the countryside.

Understand and apply reading strategies
- Read Chapter 1 together, taking turns to read aloud. Ask children to predict what might have happened to Father and where he might have gone.
- Reread pp6–7. Ask children to close their eyes and imagine that they're Bobbie. Help them to develop empathy by questioning them about their feelings.
- Ask children to read on to find out what will happen to the children as their lives change.